ADDING & SUBTRACTING PUZZLES

Karen Bryant-Mole

Designed and illustrated by Graham Round

Edited by Robyn Gee

Series editor: Jenny Tyler

Adding and subtracting

Adding is when you join two or more numbers together to find out how much they make altogether. In problems the sign for addition is a cross, like the one below.

The words "plus" and "and" can also mean add.

Subtraction is when you take one number away from another. The sign for subtraction is a short line, like the one below.

The words "take away", "less" and "minus" also mean subtract.

Can you write out the correct mathematical problems to go with each of the word problems below? Write each one just like the example, which has been done for you.

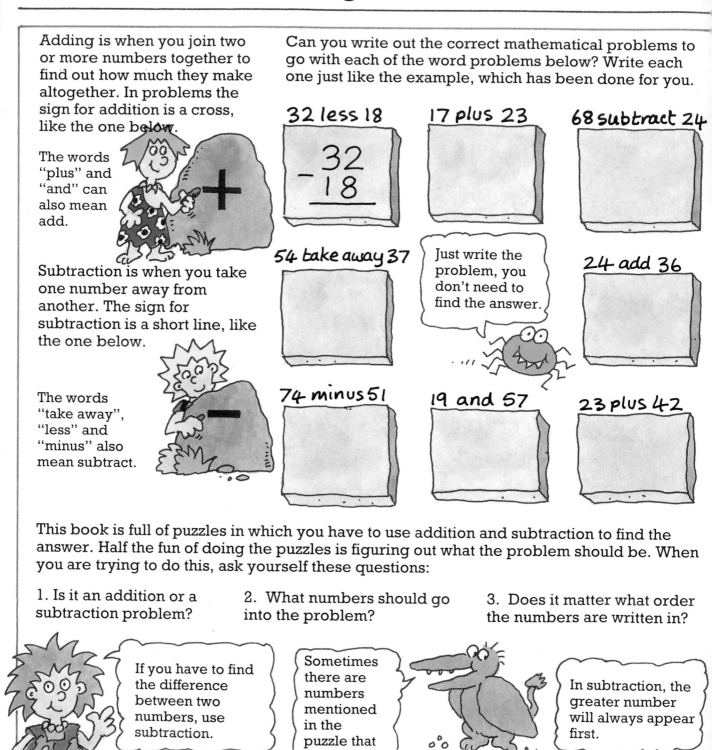

32 less 18

$$-\frac{\begin{array}{r} 32 \\ 18 \end{array}}{}$$

17 plus 23

68 subtract 24

54 take away 37

Just write the problem, you don't need to find the answer.

24 add 36

74 minus 51

19 and 57

23 plus 42

This book is full of puzzles in which you have to use addition and subtraction to find the answer. Half the fun of doing the puzzles is figuring out what the problem should be. When you are trying to do this, ask yourself these questions:

1. Is it an addition or a subtraction problem?

2. What numbers should go into the problem?

3. Does it matter what order the numbers are written in?

If you have to find the difference between two numbers, use subtraction.

If you need to find the total, use addition.

Sometimes there are numbers mentioned in the puzzle that aren't needed in the problem.

In subtraction, the greater number will always appear first.

When you have finished a puzzle you can check your answer in the Answers section on pages 28 to 32.

In this book you will meet a family called the Ogs and their friends. They live on Reptile Road, in Ogtown. Zog and Mog Og are playing with their friends. They have all been collecting smooth round stones to use as marbles. The table below tells you how many "marbles" each child has collected.

Zog	Mog	Tig
24	18	36
Mig	Heg	Deg
17	9	23

Can you figure out what problem would give you the answer to these questions?

Mig loses 4 of her marbles in a game with Mog. How many does she have now?

You don't have to find the answer. Just write the problem on the slate next to the question.

How many marbles have Mig and Tig altogether?

How many fewer marbles has Zog than Tig?

If Zog gives Deg 7 marbles, how many will he have left?

How many will Deg have, after Zog has given him 7?

Heg wins 8 more marbles. How many does she have now?

How many more marbles has Mog than Heg?

3

Meet the Og family

Grandma Og

Grandma Og loves knitting. When she counts the stitches, she prefers to count in tens.

Grandpa Og

Grandpa Og enjoys playing darts. He has the habit of counting backward.

Mrs. Og

Mrs. Og enjoys ice skating. When she counts, she leaves out every fifth number.

Mr. Og

Mr. Og is a fan of bodyball games. When he counts, he always says any number with a 6 or a 9 in it twice.

Mog Og

Mog Og likes going on picnics, particularly in Fern Forest. When she counts, she only says the even numbers.

Zog Og

Zog Og likes winter sports. He is delighted when it snows. When he counts, he says "Buzz", instead of every third number.

Each member of the family is counting the number of pebbles in his or her money box. Can you decide who said what?

Write the correct name under each speech bubble, and then continue the counting sequence by writing the next six numbers or words.

1, 2, 3, 4, 6, 7, 8, 9, 11, __ __ __ __ __

_____

1, 2, buzz, 4, 5, buzz, 7, __ __ __ __ __ __

_____

10, 20, 30, 40, 50, __ __ __ __ __ __

_____

2, 4, 6, 8, 10, 12, 14, __ __ __ __ __ __

_____

15, 16, 16, 17, 18, 19, 19, 20, 21, 22, 23, __ __ __ __ __ __

_____

21, 20, 19, 18, 17, 16, 15, __ __ __ __ __ __

_____

The Ogtown Bank

The people of Ogtown use pebbles, feathers and bones as money.

The pebble is their smallest unit of money. A feather has the same value as 10 pebbles. A bone has the same value as 10 feathers, or 100 pebbles.

The cashier at the bank is exchanging groups of pebbles for bones, feathers and pebbles. She has done the first group, can you help her with the rest?

bone   **feather**   **pebble**

10 ● = 1 feather

10 feather = 1 bone

100 ● = 1 bone

352	● =	3	5	2
834	● =			
370	● =			
25	● =			

The bone bag shows the number of hundreds, because there are 100 pebbles in one bone.

The feather bag shows the number of tens, because every 10 pebbles makes one feather.

The pebble bag shows the number of units, or ones.

Mog wants to know how many bones, feathers and pebbles she will get in exchange for her money.

This is more difficult, because sometimes she has feathers to exchange and sometimes pebbles.

Remember: 10 feathers have the same value as 1 bone, so 13 feathers is the same as 1 bone, 3 feathers and 0 pebbles.

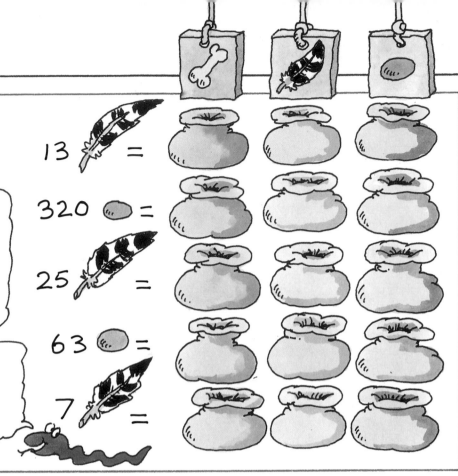

13 🪶 $=$

320 ⚫ $=$

25 🪶 $=$

63 ⚫ $=$

7 🪶 $=$

Zog has been saving up his pocket money. He now has 43 pebbles. He wants to exchange his pebbles for as many feathers as possible. How many feathers will he get? How many pebbles will he have left over?

Mr. Og is helping at tomorrow's Ogtown Fair. He knows he will need plenty of change. He wants to exchange 4 bones, 6 feathers and 7 pebbles for pebbles. How many pebbles will he have?

It was Mog Og's birthday last week. Several people gave her money. She has 166 pebbles which she wants to exchange for bones, feathers and pebbles. How many will she have of each?

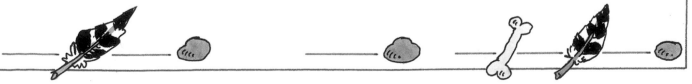

7

The Ogtown Fair

children 2 pebbles
adults 4 pebbles

It is the day of the Ogtown Annual Fair. The Ogs have come with their friends, the Igs. Mig and Tig, the Ig children, are riding on the merry-go-round. Mig paid for both of them. How much did it cost her?

_____ pebbles

Grandma Og and Mog Og are on the merry-go-round too. How much did they have to pay altogether?

_____ pebbles

How much will it cost Grandpa to buy a ticket for himself and a ticket for Grandma?

_____ pebbles

Add the spots

Mr. Og has a basket containing cards. Each card has between one and nine spots on it. You have to pick two cards. If the number of spots on both cards adds up to 10, you win a pet lizard.

On the board next to Mr. Og are several pairs of cards. He wants to show everyone which combinations of cards add up to 10. He has already drawn in one combination. Can you help him by drawing dots on the cards to show which other pairs of numbers add up to ten?

10 spots =

[card: 4 spots] and [card: 6 spots]

and

and

and

and

burger	7
hot dog	6
orange juice	5
milk	7

Zog Og has 11 pebbles. He wants to buy something to eat and something to drink. Mark the things he can afford.

Roll-a-pebble

Mrs. Og, Mrs. Ig and the children's teacher, Miss Spell, are all playing Roll-a-pebble. The purple squares are worth seven points, the pink squares are worth eight points and the orange squares are worth six points.

You roll two pebbles, look at the value of the squares they land on and add them up. If you get 15 points, you get your pebbles back. If you get 16 points, you win 5 pebbles.

Mrs. Og's pebbles have an "O" for Og on them. Has she won anything?

Look at the other pairs of pebbles. Have Mrs. Ig or Miss Spell won anything?

9

Stone Age darts

Grandma and Grandpa Og are at the Hadrosaur's Head playing darts. In this game, each player starts with 101 points. The winner is the first player to get down to 0 points. Grandma and Grandpa take turns throwing a dart. They subtract whatever number it lands on from their score.

Grandma's first dart landed on 20. 101 take away 20 equals 81, so that took her down to 81 points. Then she threw a 5. How many points did she have left? Write the answer on the scoreboard.

Grandpa's first dart landed on 14, leaving him with 87 points. He has just thrown a 17. How many points does he have left? Write the answer on the scoreboard.

The last game

Here are the points that Grandma and Grandpa scored in their last game. Can you fill in the numbers missing from the scoreboard?

Who won the match? Write "winner" at the bottom of the winner's board.

	Grandma	Grandpa
1st throw	13	16
2nd throw	12	18
3rd throw	15	10
4th throw	8	19
5th throw	11	20
6th throw	7	3
7th throw	14	15

Grandma 101 81

Grandpa 101 87

Grandma 101

Grandpa 101

Grandpa is now down to 45 points. Before his last turn he had 63 points. What did he score with his last dart? Draw his dart in the correct place on the dartboard.

63
−45

To figure out what he scored with his last dart, you need to find the difference between the two numbers.

To figure out the difference between two numbers, you take the smaller number away from the bigger number.

Look at these pairs of scores below and see if you can decide what number the last dart landed on.

Use the notebooks to figure out the score and then draw a dart in the correct place on the dartboard.

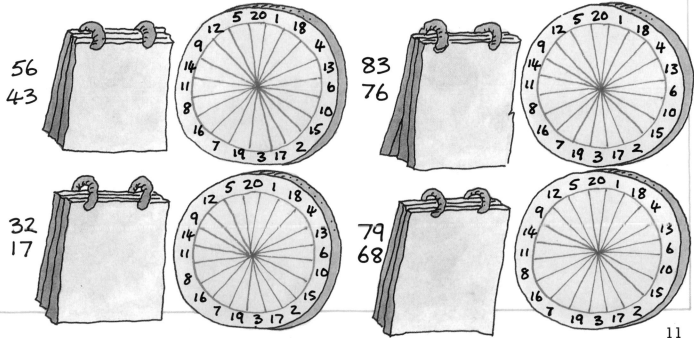

56
43

83
76

32
17

79
68

Treasure hunt

Mr. Slug, one of the teachers at Ogtown School, has organized a treasure hunt for Mog's class to follow, instead of having their afternoon lessons today. There are lots of treasure chests, but only one has a prize inside it. To find their way to the prize, the children have to take the correct paths.

At each junction they come to, they have to find the answer to a subtraction problem. They then follow the path which shows that number. To make it a bit more difficult they can only discover what the answer is by solving some clues.

Mog and Zog have already figured out the first problem. Can you help them do the rest and win the prize?

There are 14 days in a fortnight and 2 socks in a pair:

14 - 2 = 12

We follow the path marked 12.

The number of days in a fortnight, minus the number of socks in a pair.

The number of legs on an octopus, minus the number of corners in a square.

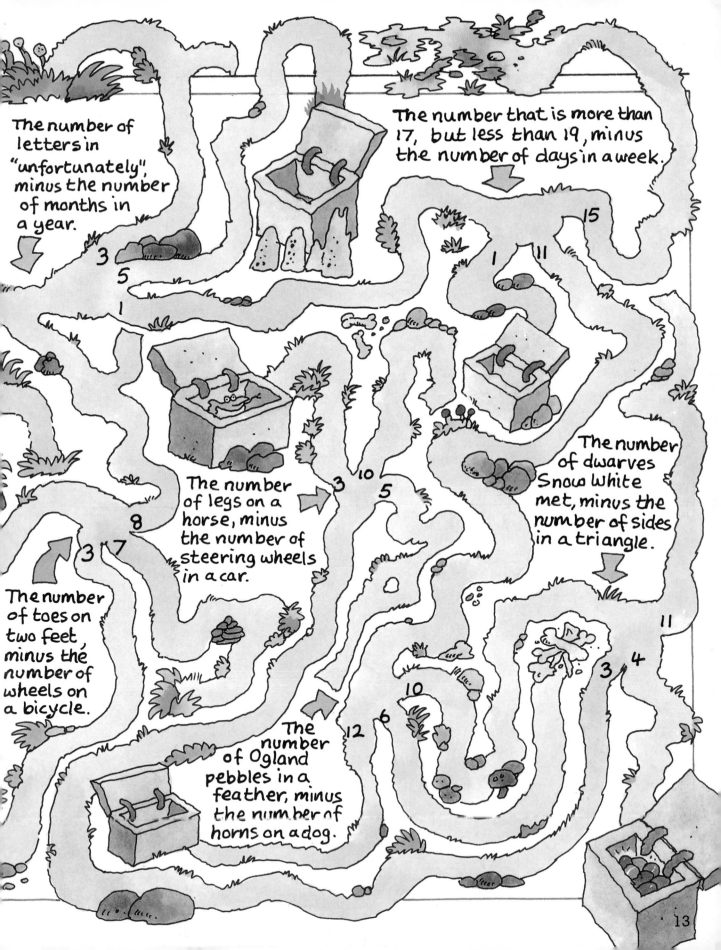

The number of letters in "unfortunately", minus the number of months in a year.

The number that is more than 17, but less than 19, minus the number of days in a week.

The number of legs on a horse, minus the number of steering wheels in a car.

The number of dwarves Snow White met, minus the number of sides in a triangle.

The number of toes on two feet, minus the number of wheels on a bicycle.

The number of Ogland pebbles in a feather, minus the number of horns on a dog.

13

The Ogtown superstore

This abacus shows the price of a dozen free-range lizard eggs - 253 pebbles.

On Saturdays, Zog sometimes works in the Ogtown superstore. Today, he is working at the check-out.

He uses an abacus to add up the price of the goods for each customer. His abacus has three columns. He puts beads on the columns to show the price of each item.

The prices in the superstore are all given in pebbles. The column on the right shows the number of ones or units; the middle column shows the tens; the column on the left shows the hundreds.

Write the price

Yesterday, Zog had to write price labels for some of the items. Each of these abacuses shows what price the item below it should be. Can you write the price in pebbles of each item on its label?

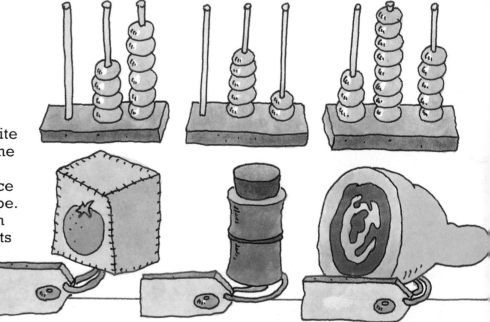

Can you help Zog add the cost of the items in each basket? You could either add the numbers on a piece of paper and then draw in the beads, or, you could add on the abacus.

If you have ten beads in the units column, erase them and draw a bead in the tens column.

If you have ten beads in the tens column, erase them and draw a bead in the hundreds column.

To add on the abacus, draw in the correct number of beads for the first item, then draw in the cost of the next item.

The lost receipts

Three customers have dropped their receipts. Can you find out which receipt belongs to which basket? Write "red", "blue" or "yellow" on each receipt to match its basket.

The bodyball game

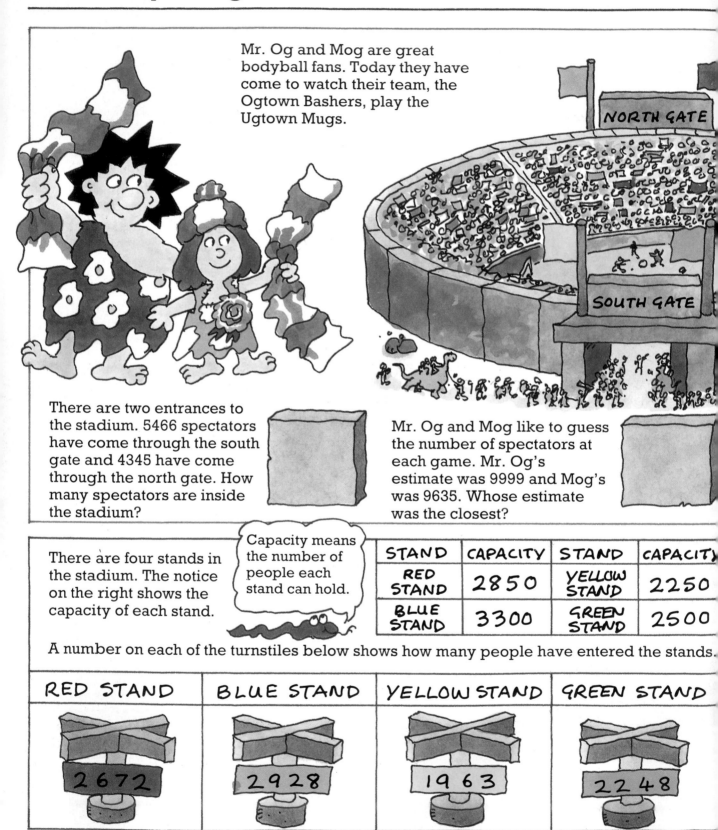

Mr. Og and Mog are great bodyball fans. Today they have come to watch their team, the Ogtown Bashers, play the Ugtown Mugs.

NORTH GATE

SOUTH GATE

There are two entrances to the stadium. 5466 spectators have come through the south gate and 4345 have come through the north gate. How many spectators are inside the stadium?

Mr. Og and Mog like to guess the number of spectators at each game. Mr. Og's estimate was 9999 and Mog's was 9635. Whose estimate was the closest?

There are four stands in the stadium. The notice on the right shows the capacity of each stand.

Capacity means the number of people each stand can hold.

STAND	CAPACITY	STAND	CAPACITY
RED STAND	2850	YELLOW STAND	2250
BLUE STAND	3300	GREEN STAND	2500

A number on each of the turnstiles below shows how many people have entered the stands.

RED STAND	BLUE STAND	YELLOW STAND	GREEN STAND
2672	2928	1963	2248

CARS

The stadium has parking space for 5000 cars. There are 4251 cars parked there at the moment. A sign at the entrance tells the motorists how many spaces are left. Draw a ring around the sign which shows the correct answer.

2 5 1
SPACES

5 5 9
SPACES

7 4 9
SPACES

Watching bodyball makes Mog hungry. She decides to buy a brontoburger. So far the burger seller has sold 1224 brontoburgers, 785 tyrannoburgers and 643 vegetarian swampburgers.

Body ball Match Notes
May 10
The _____ stand can hold the most people.
The total capacity of the stadium is _____.
The _____ stand has the fewest empty seats.

Can you fill in the gaps in Mog's notebook?

How many burgers has he sold altogether?

How many more meat burgers than vegetarian burgers has he sold?

The Ogland Winter Olympics

In winter, Ichthyosaur Lake, near Ogtown, freezes over. Here, the Ogland Winter Olympics are being held. Mrs. Og enjoys ice skating and she has come to watch the figure skating championships.

Each competitor is watched by a team of 7 judges who award points. Most skaters score between 6 and 7 points.

The number that comes after the decimal point tells you how many tenths of a whole number there are. The number 6.2 is the same as 6 whole numbers and 2 tenths.

6 and 7 are both whole numbers. To write a number that comes between two whole numbers, you need to use a decimal point and put a number after it, like this: 6.2.

Can you use the information below to find out how many points each judge gave and finish the chart?

• Judge D's score was in between that awarded by Judge C and Judge F.
• Judge A awarded a score that was 3 tenths less than Judge D.
• Judge E's score was in between that of Judge A and C.
• Judge B awarded a score that was 1 tenth lower than any so far.
• Judge G awarded a score that was 1 tenth higher than anyone else's.

This is the ice skater, Lavender Bag. Judge C awarded her 6.6 points. Judge F awarded her 6.8 points, as you can see on the scoreboard below.

A	B	C	D	E	F	G
		6.6			6.8	

Mrs. Og thinks she would have given Lavender 6.7 points. Did any of the judges agree with her?

Zog likes the bobsled races, held in the Mega Mountains, best. The bobsleds race down the course in about 45 seconds.

There is so little difference between their times, that tenths of a second are not precise enough. They have to be measured in hundredths of a second.

Bobsled	Time in seconds	Place
RESULTS		
	45.34	

Remember, the faster the bobsled, the fewer the number of seconds it takes to come down.

To write hundredths of a whole number you have to write 2 numbers after the decimal point.

45.64 can be thought of as 45 whole numbers, 6 tenths and 4 hundredths, or as 45 whole numbers and 64 hundredths.

The blue sled goes first. It takes 45.34 seconds. Can you use the information below to help you fill in the rest of the times on the results board?
• The green sled goes next. It is 5 hundredths of a second faster than the blue sled.
• Next down the track is the red sled. It is one whole second slower than the green sled.

• The yellow sled follows the red one. It is 2 tenths of a second slower than the blue sled.
• The purple sled is 3 hundredths of a second slower than the green sled.
• The last sled is orange. It is 4 hundredths of a second faster than the yellow sled.

The winning sled is the one that comes down the track in the fastest time. Which sled wins? Write "1st" in the correct space in the place column of the results board. Can you fill in the rest of the places on the results board?

19

Mog's Olympics

Mog enjoyed the Ogland Winter Olympics so much that she decided to organize her own winter sports competitions. An ice skating competition is taking place on a frozen pond in Primate Park. Grandma and Grandpa Og are the judges.

Mrs. Og skated first. Grandma gave her 6.7 points. Grandpa gave her 6.6 points. Mrs. Og's total score was 13.3 points.

You add decimals in the same way as whole numbers. Always start with the column on the far right.

Don't forget to put in the decimal point.

Medal Winners

Mog is skating now. Grandma and Grandpa are holding up the points they have awarded her. What is Mog's total score?

Mog's friend, Sally, skates after Mog. Grandma gives her 6.4 points. Grandpa gives her 6.8 points. What was her total?

Grandpa presents Mog, Sally and Mrs. Og with medals. The person with the highest score receives a gold medal; the person with the second highest score receives a silver medal; the person with the lowest score receives a bronze medal. Can you color the medals to show which contestant won which medal? Use yellow for gold, gray for silver and brown for bronze.

The fastest time ever recorded down this bobsled run is 4.75 seconds. Mrs. Ig is the timekeeper.

Don't forget - the fewer number of seconds it takes, the faster the run.

Think carefully about this.

Mr. Og had a practice run and came down the hill in 4.83 seconds. How much faster than this must he go to beat the record?

When Mr. Og takes his turn he is 0.12 seconds faster than his practice run. Does he beat the record?

First down the hill was Zog Og. His run took 5.26 seconds. How much slower than the record is this?

Mig Ig is going down the hill now. The best she has ever done is 5.42 seconds. She beats her personal best by 0.14 seconds. Is this faster or slower than Zog's run?

Each competitor has two runs down the hill. The competition is judged on the best of these two times. Fill in the times for the first run. The times for the second run have already been filled in.
    Draw a ring around each competitor's faster time. Write 1st, 2nd or 3rd to show what order they came in.

Name	1st run	2nd run	Place
Mr. Og		4.95	
Mig Ig		5.27	
Zog Og		5.30	

Palm Bay

Mr. and Mrs. Og, Zog and Mog are off for a two week break on the sunny island of Palm Bay. There is a time difference of one hour between Ogtown and Palm Bay. Palm Bay is one hour ahead.

When it is 4 o'clock in Palm Bay it is only 3 o'clock in Ogtown.

There are 60 minutes in one hour.

Here is Mrs. Og's plane ticket. Can you figure out how long the journey actually takes and fill in the space on the ticket?

Name: Mrs. Og
Destination: Palm Bay
Departure: 11:00am (local time)
Arrival: 3:30pm (local time)
Journey time:
Please check in 1½ hours before departure

This means that it will be 11 o'clock in Ogtown when they leave.

This means that it will be 3:30 in Palm Bay when they arrive.

Time plan

Mr. Og wants to make sure that they will not be late for the plane, so he is making a time plan. Can you write in the times for him? Use the information below to help you.

• They must be at the airport to check in their luggage one and a half hours before departure.

• The journey time to the airport by taxi is 45 minutes.

• Mr. Og allows an extra 20 minutes, in case there are delays on the way.

• He allows one hour for everyone to get dressed and eat breakfast.

PLAN	TIME
Must be at the airport by:	
Must leave Ogtown by:	
Call taxi by:	
Set alarm for:	

It is 10 past 4 by the time they have collected their suitcases and found the bus that will take them to their hotel. The bus journey takes 25 minutes.

Draw a ring around the clock that shows the time they arrive at their hotel.

| 4:15 | 4:35 | 5:10 |

Later that evening, they telephone Grandma and Grandpa to let them know they have arrived safely. Look at the time on the clock in the hotel and then draw the hands on the clock in the Og's house.

Don't forget the time difference.

Before going to bed, Mog writes about the day's events in her diary. Can you fill in the missing times?

May 22nd.
Arrived in Palm Bay.
The whole journey took
_____ hours _____
minutes but we were
only actually moving
in vehicles for _____
hours and _____
minutes.

Mog and Zog's homework

Miss Spell, Mog and Zog's teacher, has asked them both to do some math problems at home and bring them to school to show her.

Mog and Zog's baby cousin, Fossil, came to stay the night. Unfortunately, she got into Zog's room and smashed up all his homework rocks. Can you write each problem again, in the right order, on Zog's spare homework rocks?

There are two ways of writing each problem, but you only need to find one.

67 = 44 +

23

+

22

59

=

37

58 − 45

13

=

3 7

= 54

85 31 −

2

× 5

Mog is doing some subtraction for her homework. She wants to make sure she did them all right, so she is going to check them.

She knows that she can check them by adding back in the number that she took away. If the number she gets is the same as the first number in the problem, her answer is correct.

Can you finish checking Mog's problems? Put a check next to the correct answers and a cross next to the wrong answers.

These two are the same, so Mog's answer is right.

These two are different, so Mog knows she has made a mistake.

$$\begin{array}{c} \circled{67} \\ -21 \\ \hline 46 \\ +21 \checkmark \\ \hline \circled{67} \end{array} \qquad \begin{array}{c} \circled{56} \\ -34 \\ \hline 32 \\ +34 \times \\ \hline \circled{66} \end{array}$$

$$\begin{array}{c} 97 \\ -54 \\ \hline 32 \end{array} \qquad \begin{array}{c} 38 \\ -6 \\ \hline 32 \end{array}$$

$$\begin{array}{c} 43 \\ -12 \\ \hline 35 \end{array} \qquad \begin{array}{c} 86 \\ -23 \\ \hline 63 \end{array}$$

$$\begin{array}{c} 77 \\ -55 \\ \hline 22 \end{array} \qquad \begin{array}{c} 52 \\ -21 \\ \hline 31 \end{array}$$

Stepping stones

Mog and Zog want to collect mushrooms in Fern Forest. To get there they have to cross Smelly Swamp, which is guarded by the cunning swamp creatures.

These creatures make up a different puzzle every day and you can only cross the swamp by solving the puzzle correctly.

Today, Mog and Zog have to decide what symbol and number should go on the blue stepping stones. If it is an addition sign and a number, they go forward that number of stepping stones. If it is a take away sign, they go back that number of stones.

If they solve the puzzle correctly they will end up at Fern Forest. Can you help them?

They should always land on a blue stepping stone.

Mog and Zog have solved the first part of the puzzle.

The missing symbol is + and the missing number is 4.

To help you solve the puzzle, put a coin or counter on "start" and move forward 4 places.

When you have figured out the next problem, write the sign and the number on the stone and then move your counter.

26

Answers

Page 2

32 less 18
$$\begin{array}{r} 32 \\ -18 \end{array}$$

17 plus 23
$$\begin{array}{r} 17 \\ +23 \end{array}$$

68 subtract 24
$$\begin{array}{r} 68 \\ -24 \end{array}$$

54 take away 37
$$\begin{array}{r} 54 \\ -37 \end{array}$$

Just write the problem, you don't need to find the answer.

24 add 36
$$\begin{array}{r} 24 \\ +36 \end{array}$$

74 minus 51
$$\begin{array}{r} 74 \\ -51 \end{array}$$

19 and 57
$$\begin{array}{r} 19 \\ +57 \end{array}$$

23 plus 42
$$\begin{array}{r} 23 \\ +42 \end{array}$$

Page 3

In this book you will meet a family called the Ogs and their friends. They live on Reptile Road, in Ogtown. Zog and Mog Og are playing with their friends. They have all been collecting smooth round stones to use as marbles. The table below tells you how many "marbles" each child has collected.

Zog	Mog	Tig
24	18	36
Mig	Heg	Deg
17	9	23

Can you figure out what problem would give you the answer to these questions?

You don't have to find the answer. Just write the problem on the slate next to the question.

Mig loses 4 of her marbles in a game with Mog. How many does she have now?
$$\begin{array}{r} 17 \\ -4 \end{array}$$

$$\begin{array}{r} 36 \\ -24 \end{array}$$

$$\begin{array}{r} 36 \\ +17 \end{array} \text{ OR } \begin{array}{r} 17 \\ +36 \end{array}$$

$$\begin{array}{r} 24 \\ -7 \end{array}$$

How many will Deg have, after Zog has given him 7?
$$\begin{array}{r} 23 \\ +7 \end{array} \text{ OR } \begin{array}{r} 7 \\ +23 \end{array}$$

$$\begin{array}{r} 9 \\ +8 \end{array} \text{ OR } \begin{array}{r} 8 \\ +9 \end{array}$$

$$\begin{array}{r} 18 \\ -9 \end{array}$$

Page 5

Each member of the family is counting the number of pebbles in his or her money box. Can you decide who said what?

Write the correct name under each speech bubble, and then continue the counting sequence by writing the next six numbers or words.

1, 2, 3, 4, 6, 7, 8, 9, 11, 12, 13, 14, 16, 17, 18
Mrs. Og

1, 2, buzz, 4, 5, buzz, 7, 8, buzz 10, 11 buzz 13
Zog

10, 20, 30, 40, 50, 60, 70, 80, 90, 100, 110
Grandma

2, 4, 6, 8, 10, 12, 14, 16, 18, 20, 22, 24, 26
Mog

15, 16, 16, 17, 18, 19, 19, 20, 21, 22, 23, 24, 25, 26, 26, 27, 28
Mr. Og

21, 20, 19, 18, 17, 16, 15, 14, 13, 12, 11, 10, 9
Grandpa

Pages 6 and 7

The people of Ogtown use pebbles, feathers and bones as money.
The pebble is their smallest unit of money. A feather has the same value as 10 pebbles. A bone has the same value as 10 feathers, or 100 pebbles.
The cashier at the bank is exchanging groups of pebbles for bones, feathers and pebbles. She has done the first group, can you help her with the rest?

bone	feather	pebble
10	= 1	
10		= 1
100	= 1	

352	=	3	5	2
834	=	8	3	4
370	=	3	7	0
25	=	0	2	5

The pebble bag shows the number of units, or ones.

The bone bag shows the number of hundreds, because there are 100 pebbles in one bone.

The feather bag shows the number of tens, because every 10 pebbles makes one feather.

Mog wants to know how many bones, feathers and pebbles she will get in exchange for her money.

This is more difficult, because sometimes she has feathers to exchange and sometimes pebbles.

13 feathers = 1 3 0
320 pebbles = 3 2 0
25 feathers = 2 5 0
63 pebbles = 0 6 3
170 feathers = 7 0 0

Remember: 10 feathers have the same value as 1 bone, so 13 feathers is the same as 1 bone, 3 feathers and 0 pebbles.

Zog has been saving up his pocket money. He now has 43 pebbles. He wants to exchange his pebbles for as many feathers as possible. How many feathers will he get? How many pebbles will he have left over?
4 feathers 3

Mr. Og is helping at tomorrow's Ogtown Fair. He knows he will need 'plenty of change. He wants to exchange 4 bones, 6 feathers and 7 pebbles for pebbles. How many pebbles will he have?
467

It was Mog Og's birthday last week. Several people gave her money. She has 166 pebbles which she wants to exchange for bones, feathers and pebbles. How many will she have of each?
1 bone 6 feathers 6 pebbles

Page 8

It is the day of the Ogtown Annual Fair. The Ogs have come with their friends, the Igs. Mig and Tig, the Ig children, are riding on the merry-go-round. Mig paid for both of them. How much did it cost her?
4 pebbles

Grandma Og and Mog Og are on the merry-go-round too. How much did they have to pay altogether?
6 pebbles

How much will it cost Grandpa to buy a ticket for himself and a ticket for Grandma?
8 pebbles

children 2 pebbles
adults 4 pebbles

Add the spots

Mr. Og has a basket containing cards. Each card has between one and nine spots on it. You have to pick two cards. If the number of spots on both cards adds up to 10, you win a pet lizard.
On the board next to Mr. Og are several pairs of cards. He wants to show everyone which combinations of cards add up to 10. He has already drawn in one combination. Can you help him by drawing dots on the cards to show which other pairs of numbers add up to ten?

Your pairs of cards might be in a different order.

10 spots =

[card] and [card]
[card] and [card]
[card] and [card]
[card] and [card]
[card] and [card]

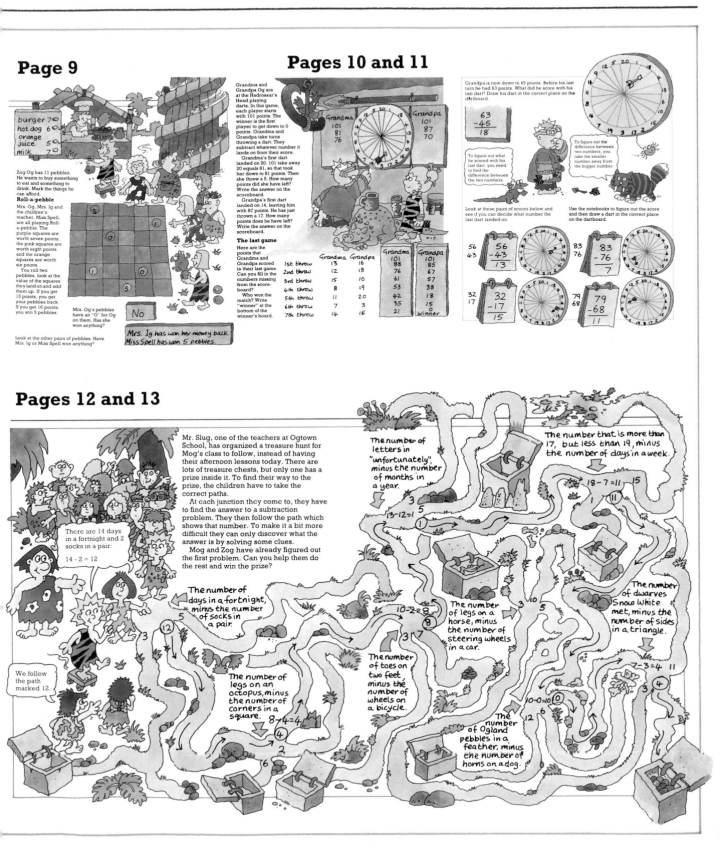

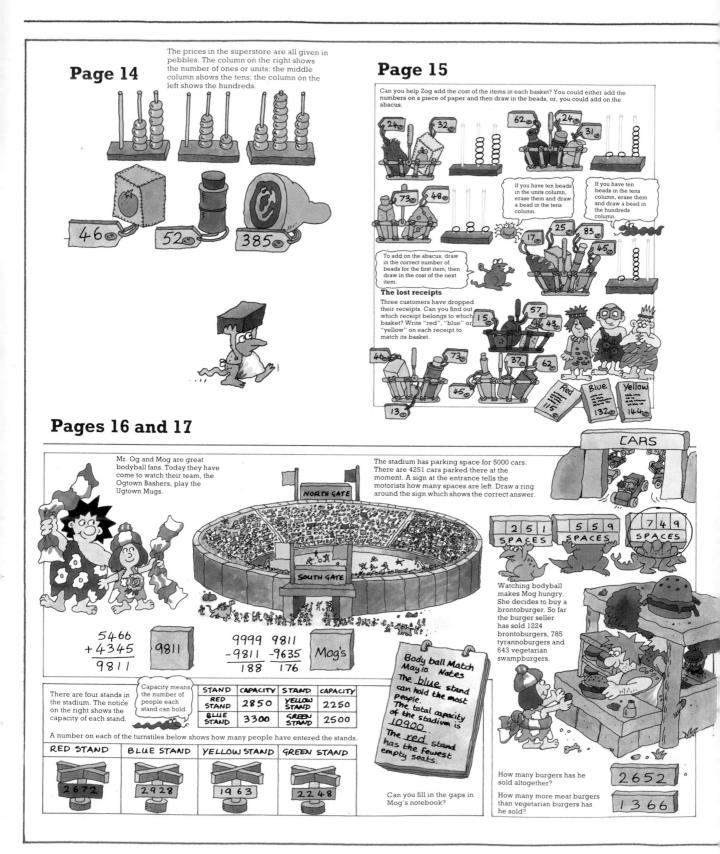

Page 14

The prices in the superstore are all given in pebbles. The column on the right shows the number of ones or units; the middle column shows the tens; the column on the left shows the hundreds.

46 52 385

Page 15

Can you help Zog add the cost of the items in each basket? You could either add the numbers on a piece of paper and then draw in the beads, or, you could add on the abacus.

24 32 62 24 31

73 48 17 25 83 45

If you have ten beads in the units column, erase them and draw a bead in the tens column.

If you have ten beads in the tens column, erase them and draw a bead in the hundreds column.

To add on the abacus, draw in the correct number of beads for the first item, then draw in the cost of the next item.

The lost receipts

Three customers have dropped their receipts. Can you find out which receipt belongs to which basket? Write "red", "blue" or "yellow" on each receipt to match its basket.

57 43 15 46 73 37 62 45 13

Red 115 Blue 132 Yellow 144

Pages 16 and 17

Mr. Og and Mog are great bodyball fans. Today they have come to watch their team, the Ogtown Bashers, play the Ugtown Mugs.

NORTH GATE SOUTH GATE

The stadium has parking space for 5000 cars. There are 4251 cars parked there at the moment. A sign at the entrance tells the motorists how many spaces are left. Draw a ring around the sign which shows the correct answer.

CARS

251 SPACES   559 SPACES   749 SPACES

Watching bodyball makes Mog hungry. She decides to buy a brontoburger. So far the burger seller has sold 1224 brontoburgers, 785 tyrannoburgers and 643 vegetarian swampburgers.

$$\begin{array}{r} 5466 \\ +4345 \\ \hline 9811 \end{array}$$

9811

$$\begin{array}{r} 9999 \\ -9811 \\ \hline 188 \end{array} \qquad \begin{array}{r} 9811 \\ -9635 \\ \hline 176 \end{array}$$

Mog's

There are four stands in the stadium. The notice on the right shows the capacity of each stand.

Capacity means the number of people each stand can hold.

STAND	CAPACITY	STAND	CAPACITY
RED STAND	2850	YELLOW STAND	2250
BLUE STAND	3300	GREEN STAND	2500

A number on each of the turnstiles below shows how many people have entered the stands.

RED STAND	BLUE STAND	YELLOW STAND	GREEN STAND
2672	2928	1963	2248

Body ball Match May 10 Notes
The blue stand can hold the most people.
The total capacity of the stadium is 10900.
The red stand has the fewest empty seats.

Can you fill in the gaps in Mog's notebook?

How many burgers has he sold altogether? 2652

How many more meat burgers than vegetarian burgers has he sold? 1366

Page 18

In winter, Ichthyosaur Lake, near Ogtown, freezes over. Here, the Ogland Winter Olympics are being held. Mrs. Og enjoys ice skating and she has come to watch the figure skating championships.

Each competitor is watched by a team of 7 judges who award points. Most skaters score between 6 and 7 points.

The number that comes after the decimal point tells you how many tenths of a whole number there are. The number 6.2 is the same as 6 whole numbers and 2 tenths.

6 and 7 are both whole numbers. To write a number that comes between two whole numbers, you need to use a decimal point and put a number after it, like this: 6.2.

Can you use the information below to find out how many points each judge gave and finish the chart?
- Judge D's score was in between that awarded by Judge C and Judge F.
- Judge A awarded a score that was 3 tenths less than Judge D.
- Judge E's score was in between that of Judge A and C.
- Judge B awarded a score that was 1 tenth lower than any so far.
- Judge G awarded a score that was 1 tenth higher than anyone else's.

This is the ice skater, Lavender Bag. Judge C awarded her 6.6 points. Judge F awarded her 6.8 points, as you can see on the scoreboard below.

A	B	C	D	E	F	G
6.4	6.3	6.6	6.7	6.5	6.8	6.9

Mrs. Og thinks she would have given Lavender 6.7 points. Did any of the judges agree with her?

Yes, Judge D

Page 19

RESULTS		
Bobsled	Time in seconds	Place
🛷	45.34	3rd
🛷	45.29	1st
🛷	46.29	6th
🛷	45.54	5th
🛷	45.32	2nd
🛷	45.50	4th

Page 20

Mog enjoyed the Ogland Winter Olympics so much that she decided to organize her own winter sports competitions. An ice skating competition is taking place on a frozen pond in Primate Park. Grandma and Grandpa Og are the judges.

Mrs. Og skated first. Grandma gave her 6.7 points. Grandpa gave her 6.6 points. Mrs. Og's total score was 13.3 points.

You add decimals in the same way as whole numbers. Always start with the column on the far right.

Don't forget to put in the decimal point.

$$\begin{array}{r} 6.7 \\ +6.6 \\ \hline 13.1 \end{array}$$ 13.1

$$\begin{array}{r} 6.4 \\ +6.8 \\ \hline 13.2 \end{array}$$ 13.2

1st - Gold
2nd - Silver
3rd - Bronze

Page 21

The fastest time ever recorded down this bobsled run is 4.75 seconds. Mrs. Ig is the timekeeper.

Don't forget - the fewer number of seconds it takes the faster the run.

Think carefully about this.

$$\begin{array}{r} 4.83 \\ -4.75 \\ \hline 0.08 \end{array}$$ This would equal 0.08, not beat the record. 0.09

$$\begin{array}{r} 4.83 \\ -0.12 \\ \hline 4.71 \end{array}$$ Yes

$$\begin{array}{r} 5.26 \\ -4.75 \\ \hline 0.51 \end{array}$$ 0.51

$$\begin{array}{r} 5.42 \\ -0.14 \\ \hline 5.28 \end{array}$$ Slower

Each competitor has two runs down the hill. The competition is judged on the best of these two times. Fill in the times for the first run. The times for the second run have already been filled in.

Draw a ring around each competitor's faster time write 1st, 2nd or 3rd to show what order they came in.

Name	1st run	2nd run	Place
Mr. Og	(4.71)	4.95	1st
Mig Ig	5.28	(5.27)	3rd
Zoy Og	(5.26)	5.30	2nd

Page 22

Name: Mrs. Og
Destination: Palm Bay
Departure: 11:00 (local time)
Arrival: 3:30 (local time)
Journey time: 3½ hours
Please check in 1½ hours before departure

This means that it will be 11 o'clock in Ogtown when they leave.

This means that it will be 3:30 in Palm Bay when they arrive.

Time plan

Mr. Og wants to make sure that they will not be late for the plane, so he is making a time plan. Can you write in the times for him? Use the information below to help you.

- They must be at the airport to check in their luggage one and a half hours before departure.
- The journey time to the airport by taxi is 45 minutes.
- Mr. Og allows an extra 20 minutes, in case there are delays on the way.
- He allows one hour for everyone to get dressed and eat breakfast.

PLAN	TIME
Must be at the airport by:	4.30
Must leave Ogtown by:	8.45
Call taxi by:	8.25
Set alarm for:	7.25

Page 23

4:15	4:35	5:10

Later that evening, they telephone Grandma and Grandpa to let them know they have arrived safely. Look at the time on the clock in the hotel and then draw the hands on the clock in the Og's house.

Don't forget the time difference.

Before going to bed, Mog writes about the day's events in her diary. Can you fill in the missing times?

May 22nd.
Arrived in Palm Bay.
The whole journey took 7 hours 10 minutes but we were only actually moving in vehicles for 4 hours and 40 minutes.

Page 24

$67 = 44 +$

23

$23 + 44 = 67$
$\text{or } 44 + 23 = 67$

$+$

59 22

$37 =$

$37 + 22 = 59$
$\text{or } 22 + 37 = 59$

$58 - 45$ $=$

$58 - 45 = 13$
$\text{or } 58 - 13 = 45$

$=$ 31 54 $-$

85

$85 - 31 = 54$
$\text{or } 85 - 54 = 31$

3 7

2

$\times$ 5

Page 25

97	38
-54	- 6
32 ×	32 ∕
+ 54	+ 6
86	38

43	
-12	86
35 ×	-23
+12	63 ∕
47	+23
	86

77	52
-55	-21
22 ∕	31 ∕
+55	+21
77	52

Page 26 and 27

Mog and Zog want to collect mushrooms in Fern Forest. To get there they have to cross Smelly Swamp, which is guarded by the cunning swamp creatures.

These creatures make up a different puzzle every day and you can only cross the swamp by solving the puzzle correctly.

Today, Mog and Zog have to decide what symbol and number should go on the blue stepping stones. If it is an addition sign and a number, they go forward that number of stepping stones. If it is a take away sign, they go back that number of stones.

If they solve the puzzle correctly they will end up at Fern Forest. Can you help them?

They should always land on a blue stepping stone.

Mog and Zog have solved the first part of the puzzle.

The missing symbol is + and the missing number is 4.

To help you solve the puzzle, put a coin or counter on "start" and move forward 4 places.

When you have figured out the next problem, write the sign and the number on the stone and then move your counter.

$8 - 4 = 4$

$6 + 3 = 9$

$7 - 2 = 5$

Finish

$2 + 6 = 8$

$4 + 2 = 6$

$1 + 8 = 9$

Smelly swamp

Start

$2 + 4 = 6$

$3 + 5 = 8$

$5 - 2 = 3$